ALL FOR QUEEN AND COUNTRY

C.J. RICHARDSON

ALL FOR QUEEN AND COUNTRY

THOMAS HOWARD, 4TH DUKE OF NORFOLK

List of historical characters

4th Duke of Norfolk Thomas Howard – born 1536

1st Wife - Mary Fitzalan, born 1540, married 1555 aged 15

2nd Wife – Margaret Audley, born 1540, married 1558, aged 18, gave birth to 4 children.

3rd Wife – Elizabeth Dacre, born 1536, wed Thomas in 1567 and died in childbirth.

Henry Howard– Earl of Northampton – Thomas's brother

Lord Henry Scrope, his sister Margaret Howard's husband.

Lord Henry Berkeley, his sister Katherine Howard's husband.

Earl of Sussex – Thomas Radcliffe – Leader of Council of the North in York and friend of Thomas Howard.

John Foxe, childhood tutor and friend of Thomas for many years

Alexander Nowell – Dean of St Paul's Cathedral and longtime friend of Thomas

Henry Fitzalan – Earl of Arundel and Father-in-law to Thomas when married to 1st wife, Mary Fitzalan.

William Barker - Personal Secretary to Thomas Howard

Higford – Personal Secretary to Thomas Howard

Bishop of Ross – John Leslie – a close friend and supporter of Mary

Earl of Moray – illegitimate son of James V and Regent of Scotland for Mary's infant son, James VI

Lord Darnley (Henry Stuart), Mary's second husband who, was murdered.

Earl of Bothwell (James Hepburn), Mary's third husband, after he murdered Darnley.

William Maitland (Mary's Secretary of State)

Roberto Ridolfi – The Italian Baker – supporter of Mary Queen of Scots

William Cecil, Secretary of State and close advisor to Queen Elizabeth. Granted the title of Lord Burghley in 1571.

Robert Dudley - Earl of Leicester (Queen's lover)- a Privy Council member.

Ralph Sadler-Privy Councillor, Chancellor of the Duchy of Lancaster.

Sir Henry Neville – Gentleman of the Privy chamber.

Sir Francis Knollys – Privy Councillor, Vice-Chamberlain of the Household of Elizabeth, and Captain of the halberdiers.

Chapter 1

October 1568

'I FEEL AN AGUE coming on. I hope they do not have us waiting too long in this damnably cold weather,' I complained. The air was sharp against my cheeks, and I felt the usual pains building in my back and legs as I peered into the shroud of mist that enveloped us both. Ralph Sadler was one of the men the Queen had assigned to me for this disagreeable task of meeting up with the representatives of the Scottish Queen Mary about three miles outside York. He was a thickset man with a round face, wiry red hair and a beard to match.

'You should be used to it by now,' answered Ralph, 'all those years spent on the borders, fighting the Scots.'

'It is for that reason I suffer so now. Where the hell are they? I need to get into the warmth.'

As Ralph finished speaking, a large group of horsemen appeared out of the gloom a little further up the road. The Bishop of Ross, Lord Herries, and several other commissioners who supported Mary, greeted us. Without too much ceremony, we made our way quickly to the lodgings, where we were all to stay.

With the later arrival of Regent Moray and his large party of delegates, York became extraordinarily crowded, and lodgings were scarce as they took over several boarding houses.

Once we had finished eating and resting, we went to King's Manor, located just outside the city walls. My longtime friend, Sussex, who was now the Lord President of the Council of the North, awaited us there. We were meeting to discuss the casket letters and ballads belonging to the Scottish Queen, letters they professed her to have sent to Bothwell, her lover. The conference was to determine whether she was guilty of murdering her husband, Lord Darnley.

I remembered well the rumours of Darnley being a cruel husband who had Mary's private secretary David Rizzio killed through jealousy of their close friendship and how this had led to the breakdown of their marriage. Then came the news, in the following February, that Darnley was dead. The Queen called for a meeting with the privy council and told us she had received urgent news from Regent Moray that Darnley had been murdered after he stayed overnight at Kirk O' Field House in Edinburgh. An enormous explosion had destroyed the house, but Darnley had been found dead in the garden, apparently smothered. The prime suspect for what had happened was the Earl of Bothwell.

*

We gathered around the large table. Sussex, his councillors, myself, and Ralph Sadler were the first to hear the charges against Regent Moray from Bishop Ross and other of Mary's representatives. Moray was the guardian of Mary's infant son, James, and wished to remain so until the boy was old enough to rule Scotland. I made it clear to all that Sadler and I were not there to judge, but to investigate the case. 'Our duties,' I added, 'also include advice on how she might be returned to her throne in Scotland without the danger of her relapsing into misgovernment.'

From the start, both the Scottish parties were looking for signs that I might show favouritism towards the other party. I had to work hard to avoid these baseless accusations as I questioned and listened to Regent Moray and the Scottish Queen's representatives.

When the day's meeting finally ended, Regent Moray asked to speak to me privately. Swearing me to secrecy, he explained that he and his party would not like Mary accused or dishonoured for her son's cause and the respect to the right of both of them to the Crown of England.

'I am sent to hear your accusations,' I said, trying to show more patience than I felt, as my legs throbbed and I wanted only my bed. 'but neither will I, nor the Queen, my mistress, give out any sentence upon them.'

Before retiring, I sent a letter to the Queen, reporting the early issues and difficulties arising over the rival commission's terms. I told her it would likely prove a lengthy conference under such circumstances.

The following day, as the discussions continued, Moray showed me five of the Casket Letters and the ballads Mary had sent to her lover Bothwell while conspiring with him to have her husband, Lord Darnley, killed. It was difficult for me not to show the revulsion I felt as bile rushed to my throat while reading them.

I wrote to Elizabeth again, telling her that if the letters were genuine and written in Mary's hand, as I believed them to be, her involvement in the murder was indisputable.

The conference resumed, but any agreement between the parties on what should happen to Mary and whether she should be returned to the Scottish throne came to a stalemate over the next few days.

Unsure how to progress matters, I wrote to William Cecil, Secretary of State and Elizabeth's chief advisor.

*'This cause is the doubtfullest and dangerous that ever
I have dealt in. If you saw and heard the constant affirm-
ing of both sides, not without great stoutness, you would
wonder!'*

Later that day, Sussex took me to one side.

'I have had word from the Queen that she wishes for a full
Privy Council meeting in London to consider the points you
raised.'

"Tis the right conclusion,' I said, relieved I would no longer
be continuously pestered by both sides. I would be glad to be
back in the south, where the weather was a little more clement
and where I could spend time with my children, but I still had
my duties on the northern borders to attend. Still, I could now
at least get on with the task.

'I will gather them all and inform them of the Queen's
wishes,' said Sussex, nodding his agreement. 'It will be better
in the end if Her Majesty makes the final decisions.'

*

The next day, I took time to relax. Happy to join Mary's Secretary of State, William Maitland, in Cawood, some eight miles
south of York by the river Ouse, to go hawking. We had met at
the siege of Leith some years before and got on well. Secretary
Maitland, eager to renew our friendship, had invited me to
join in a day's sport. My spirits had lifted as the weather had
turned, and the day was gloriously fine.

Our conversation touched on the Casket Letters and how
the situation might be resolved as we scanned the cloudless
skies for our hawks. I squinted, shading my eyes against the
bright sun until, out of the blue, Maitland said, 'Mary could

be married off to someone who could manage her. It would certainly cut the Gordian knot.'

I turned sharply to look at Maitland. 'Who would want her?' 'Anyone with a mind to the Scottish throne,' he said, laughing. 'What about you, Norfolk? She would be restored to the Scottish throne, and in the fullness of time, she and her son would reign at Whitehall and Holyrood.' His eyes gleamed, and a smile played across his face.

I frowned, a little shocked at his proposal. 'Grief, man. I think I have had my fill of wives. I have enough children to carry my name forward. Besides, I still mourn my wife, Elizabeth. She was mine for so little time, and tis barely a year since I lost her and the child she was carrying.' Remembering made my eyes tear up, and I looked to the sky again to hide my weakness.

'Knollys thinks she should marry George Carey, Her Majesty's cousin. He says she did not mislike the idea.'

'Then mayhap she will,' I replied dismissively. 'It would most like solve the problem.

Chapter 2

October 1568

I WOKE TO A tapping sound at my door. I stirred, wincing as my back jarred in pain. Who would bother me at this hour?

'Who wakes me?' I growled.

'I have a message from the Bishop of Ross, sire. He begs your audience.'

It was early in the morning and still dark. I could not hear the comings and goings of anyone else in the rooms about me. Curious about Ross's intentions, I got dressed.

The Bishop's early visit surprised me, and I hoped it wasn't another plea for support of the Scottish Queen. He would regret waking me so early if it was so.

The Bishop was waiting in the gallery. He wore a tight-fitting skull cap, which sat high on his head, showing a long, thin nose above tight, thin lips. His beard was sparse and cut short, his eyes small and piercing. With a trembling voice, thick with the accent of his birth country, his manner appeared subservient as we exchanged formal greetings, and I had servants bring ale and a platter of bread and cheese so we might break our fast together.

Ross wasted no time in answering my thoughts. 'I have come from speaking with Secretary Maitland, Sire, and seek your opinion of my lady, Queen Mary, now that you have seen the casket letters.'

The disgust I had felt on first reading the letters returned, and I had to swallow hard. It was difficult to control my urge to send this man packing, but knowing how loyal Ross was to Mary, I searched for the words carefully and spoke kindly in response.

'My opinion does not leave me against the Scottish Queen. I bear her no ill will, but you must realise, should such matters be proved against her, it would dishonour her forever. I advise you to speak again with Maitland and try to find another way to stay the matter.'

Other commissioners were now assembling to break their fast, and Ross left, saying he would ride to Bolton to report to his mistress. I was glad to send Ross away. I would have a long journey to face the morrow and the more rest I had in advance, the better. My bones still ached after the journey from London to York. Looking through the window, I saw the weather turning bleak again, which would mean further suffering from the ague.

*

The following morning, I said my farewells to the remaining commissioners before heading north to inspect the defences on the Borders. This had all been planned with Her Majesty before the conference had been organised. I was to report on the state of the Berwick Garrison and the Scottish Marches.

I was already missing my children. When my eldest son Philip was born, I had vowed he would not follow the same path in life that my father had. Always absent from my and my siblings' lives. I could only recall us spending one brief summer with him. From the earliest years of my life, I had many memories of standing close to the windows, staring into the distance, watching, and waiting for him, and I knew him only through the reputation of his misdemeanours. Later, I learnt he had been charged with treason after he had displayed the arms of Edward the Confessor, his ancestor, in the principal quarter of his arms. I did not understand the significance of it, but was told he had been arrested and sent to the Tower before being executed. I was not allowed to visit him and was left only with paintings in the long gallery at home by which to remember him.

I was then separated from my siblings and placed with the Treasurer of the Court of Augmentations, Sir John Williams. Sir John was kept busy in London while I spent my days in isolation at his manor house near Thame. It was a joyous day, a good year later, when I was reunited with my siblings, and we were all put in the charge of our aunt, the Duchess of Richmond.

I also knew little of my grandfather. He had been a powerful man at court, but when my father was arrested, King Henry suspected my grandfather had also been involved and imprisoned him in the Tower at the same time as my father. He was charged with treason, but fortune was on his side and the night before his execution was due, Henry VIII died and the execution did not take place. I was barely eleven years old, and the closest companion for me and my siblings had been our tutor, John Foxe, whom we all loved and respected. When our grandfather came home to Kenninghall in 1553. He, being a devout Catholic, sent Foxe away and appointed a Catholic tutor.

My grandfather was restored to all his lands and properties and enjoyed power at court once more also spent much time in London. He had been reinstated as Earl Marshal, and his houses and home at Kenninghall were restored. He was a strict guardian with little sympathy for what had happened to his own son. To keep me in line, he took charge of me and relayed what had happened, with tales of torture and the terrible conditions of the Tower, which left me with nightmares and a great fear of ever being sent there. It made me wonder if he, with his strict controls, views, and opinions, had been the reason for my father's waywardness and rebellious spirit. My father had also been a celebrated poet as well as a rebel, and I would sit quietly on many occasions in a window seat to read his work. It gave me a better insight into his character, a side I could admire.

*

John Forster greeted me in Alnwick, and we discussed the troubles in the Middle Marches that had resulted in the deaths of six Englishmen. I then travelled on to other garrisons to glean which were holding well against the border reivers, and which needed further support. Each night, I made my report, making suggestions for improvements, who needed extra men, who had been killed, and what successes had been reported to me.

As October slipped into November, I wrote to London, enclosing my reports and adding,

> 'Winter is setting in, and never have I seen worse weather for snow and frost. It is much worse than the snow we sometimes suffer in Norfolk at Christmas. It is as ill a journey as ever I have had, with the most unreasonable weather ever seen in this country so early in the year. I will be glad when I can travel south once more.'

It worsened as I passed through Cumberland, and my rheumatism pained me ever more deeply. I wrote to Philip saying how much I missed him and my other children, telling them what a cold and miserable place the North was and how I longed to see them all.

Chapter 3

November to December 1568

'WHAT RUMOURS?'

'Rumours that you intend to marry the Scottish Queen,' said Cecil. 'There have been whisperings all about court while you have been in the north.'

I was furious. I was not about to confide in this man who had recently seized four Spanish treasure ships bound for the Netherlands, making him the most unpopular man in London. "'Tis a lie. I would have none of such a woman. Having seen the letters, how could I countenance such a joining? I mislike the idea much.'

I did not tell Cecil that the idea had crossed my mind while I had been away at Berwick Garrison and the Marches, gathering information and drafting reports for the Queen. Though the thought of what she had done to Darnley still repulsed me, I believed it might be not so bad. If I brought Mary under my rule as a wife, it would put paid to any plans she might have in turning England back to Catholicism and placing it under the control of the Pope in Rome. The thought of the country slipping back into papish ways would make my life miserable. I was a faithful Anglican and had been since I was a young man, hearing the views of my oldest friends, John Foxe and

Alexander Nowell. The Mary Tudor years had left me bereft when John had to flee the country.

'I am pleased to hear it,' said Cecil, breathing a sigh of relief. 'Her Majesty would speak with you on the matter when the conference is over. For now, you must join us in the Star Chamber. All oaths are done, and we hear from Bishop Ross and then Regent Moray. As you took your oaths in York, you will not be required to do so again.'

I sighed deeply. My bones still ached from the terrible cold and snow-covered lands I had traversed in the past week. I wished for nothing more than my bed, but there was little choice, and I followed Cecil into the Chamber.

Bishop Ross read his commission aloud, his manner subservient as usual. He started by apologising that it was sealed only with Mary's signet, as she had no Great Seal since leaving Scotland.

He finished by saying more forcefully, 'Her Majesty, Mary, Queen of Scotland must not be treated judicially in the respect that she is a free princess with a crown given to her by God.'

I could see the man spoke earnestly and felt a pang of pity for him; the council remained steely-faced.

When Ross had withdrawn, Regent Moray and the commissioners for Mary's infant son, King James, entered the room. Cecil asked Moray if they carried the accusation with them. Moray's secretary took the document from within his doublet and said, 'I cannot deliver the contents until the Regent has been given Her Majesty's assurance, in writing, for which he had asked at York.'

Angered by the request, the Bishop of Orkney grabbed the document from Wood's hands and passed it to Cecil.

'Well done, Bishop,' called out one of the Lords, 'thou art the frankest fellow among them all.'

Having been the one who had advised Regent Moray at the York conference, I felt my cheeks flush with guilt. At that moment, I saw the exchange of smiles and even a wink between John Wood and Cecil, leaving me a little confused. Had it all been planned in advance?

Although the damage was already done, Moray asked that the document be returned to him as he still had items to add.

'You are at liberty to send those at a later time,' said Cecil dismissively. Moray left the meeting in a temper.

Having heard all, the Council said they would report to Elizabeth all they found to be true of such lamentable deeds. If Mary were found guilty of murdering or conspiring to murder her husband, Darnley, they would either deliver her to Moray or continue to hold her captive in England. Elizabeth would then acknowledge Mary's dimission of the Crown to her son, James, and respect Moray's authority as Regent. The Council retired for the day, and I gratefully sought my rooms, exhausted and glad for my bed, but I could not fall asleep. What would it be like to be married to a queen, and a Scottish one at that? Would I be able to get past my revulsion of knowing how she had betrayed her husband? I had been fortunate to have had three marriages, been happy and content with all of them, and was most sorry for each loss.

As I lay there, my thoughts drifted back to my first marriage to Mary Fitzalan. My grandfather had arranged the wedding, as he had been my guardian. He had thought the marriage would bring together England's two most prominent Catholic families. Even though I followed my father's path regarding faith, my memory of Mary was of a sweet, delicate young girl, and I had been most happy to marry her. When she produced me a son the following year, my dearest Philip, whom I loved more than life itself, I had thought life complete. My eyes pricked with tears, remembering Mary's painful death after a childbed fever. I had barely known her before she was gone from my life.

With each marriage, my wealth had increased considerably, making me the richest man in England. My cousin Elizabeth permitted me to marry Margaret Audley, despite her faith as a Catholic. In fact, they had been the greatest of friends for many years. Her Majesty had stayed at the Chapterhouse in the days leading up to her coronation, long before I bought it and changed its name to Howard House. The Queen had made Margaret one of her two ladies of honour. My dearest Margaret, the one I would always think of as the greatest love of my life. How I wished she were still here. It still brought tears to my eyes when thinking of her passing three weeks after bearing her fourth child for me five years ago. We had grieved together when our first child, Elizabeth, had died as an infant but rejoiced together for our three further children, Thomas, Margaret, and William.

Again, there had been no argument from Her Majesty to my marrying my third wife, Elizabeth Dacre, also a Catholic. A shadow passed over me, remembering her death and that of the stillborn child only seven months after we had wed. I still could not forgive myself for not allowing her access to a Catholic priest to administer the sacraments. I thought of the three daughters and a son from her previous marriage as my own and was delighted to betroth the girls to my three sons and the boy, George, to my little daughter, Megg. No matter, it would be a few years before the ceremonies could take place. Being betrothed protected their dowries and would allow them all a comfortable life. I was looking forward to returning to Kenninghall for a rest and visiting all my children. There was nothing in my life more pleasurable than spending time with them. I settled down, content with my thoughts of family

My mind now returned to my future. Yes! The Queen had been in favour and supported my marriages, knowing it did not alter, in any way, my loyalty to her. There would be little objection, I was sure. But a Queen? Elizabeth hated Mary. Could I convince her? I drifted into an uncomfortable sleep, feeling less optimistic about my position.

*

The next day, the Council sat and discussed the evidence before them. All seemed hesitant in placing judgement on the head of a queen, but at last, they delivered the accusation against Mary. Cecil stood and read the verdict aloud.

'As Bothwell was the chief executor of Darnley's horrible and unworthy murder, we judge that the Scottish Queen, Mary, had foreknowledge as a maintainer of the evildoers.'

As the conference dragged on, King James's commissioners, behaving as if it were against their will, offered to produce the Casket Letters and other incriminating documents, swearing them to be authentic.

Bishop Ross immediately protested. 'I cannot answer to these so-called documents. That you accept such documentation without the presence of Her Majesty Queen Mary, who should be allowed to come in person to Elizabeth's presence and answer for herself, is unjust. My colleagues and I will take no further part in these mock proceedings.' With that, he and his companions left the room.

Elizabeth sent orders to put Mary in the safe custody of the Earl of Shrewsbury at Tutbury while considering her decision on the Scottish Queen's future.

I wished no harm to Mary, regardless of my disgust at the details in the Casket Letters. I earnestly believed that a marriage between myself and her was the answer. I would certainly need to keep her on a short leash, but was still convinced it was for the sake of Elizabeth and would promote peace, avoiding upheaval and revolt by the Catholic population. I knew no one could doubt my loyalty to Her Majesty; I had been most faithful since she ascended the throne; spending all those years guarding the Scottish borders, and fighting day and night, year after year, to keep my sovereign safe. I had expressed total devotion in my readiness at all times to defend Elizabeth and the country from all quarters. Undoubtedly, the Queen would understand my reasons for wanting to marry Mary. It would solve the problem in an instant. There would be no treason charges against Queen Mary, whom God had anointed, and Elizabeth could feel secure in the knowledge her throne would be protected.

Knowing Cecil to be an arch-enemy of Mary, I decided to approach Leicester as an ally in my quest to marry her. I disliked the man and thought him vain, but visited him privately, as I knew Leicester was the Queen's favourite. I also knew Leicester hated Cecil as much as I did for preventing him from winning the Queen's hand.

*

Leicester stared at me for a few moments before speaking.

'You wish me to speak to the Queen about what? To tell her that the biggest threat to her throne should be given her freedom and, not only that, but persuade her it would be for the good if you were to marry her? God's teeth, man, are you mad? Have you lost your mind completely?'

I smiled. 'No, Sir. I am completely sound of mind. Her Majesty could rest easy without fear of retaliation once she has made Mary free to marry me, nor would the Queen have to consider harming someone anointed by God. All I ask is you think on it. It would surely benefit you, too. If Mary were to marry me, Her Majesty would not be under so much pressure to accept Duc D'Anjou. Cecil constantly tries to push for a settlement on the matter. Her requirement for an heir to the throne would be less urgent, as she has named Mary's son James. I would only ask you to lay the path open for me so that I might discuss the matter and convince her of my continued loyalty and how, in marrying her, it would answer the problem of Mary.'

Leicester stroked his beard and played with his moustache. I could see that he was turning the idea over in his head. 'Mmmm. It would remove D'Anjou from impeding my plans. I might do it in return for your support in removing Cecil from the Privy Council and out of favour with the Queen. The man is driving the country to ruin.'

I agreed readily. I also wanted Cecil removed from power, as his dislike of Mary would taint his view of a suggested match, causing him to put Elizabeth against such a proposal. I had disliked Leicester much for his influence on the Queen, but for the sake of my own plans, I was prepared to join forces with this man whom the Queen doted upon and listened to on the many occasions they spent in private.

Leicester paced the room while I waited, trying to press down my irritation at the pompous ass. Even when out of sight of the Queen, he paraded himself as if he were the most handsome and desirable of men. Everyone at court knew he was the Queen's lover and had been even when his wife Amye was still alive. He had left Amye alone at home for months on end while he cavorted. I had little respect for a man who could behave in such a way, and when his wife died after falling down the stairs a few years ago, I and others at court suspected foul play, although no one could prove it.

Finally, Leicester spoke again. 'We have complaints daily to the Council from many of our countrymen. They have had their property confiscated in the Netherlands since Cecil captured the Spanish treasure ships. He is making our biggest ally, Spain, an enemy of the realm and moving us closer to our sworn enemy, France. Besides,' he added, smiling, 'Your proposal would be worth it if only to see Cecil squirm.'

Chapter 4

January to March 1569

THE PRIVY COUNCIL, MYSELF, and the Queen, all discussed the need for funds to repair and upgrade the dilapidated harbours of England. Knowing an increase in taxes would likely present a revolt, Cecil had suggested we hold a lottery, and Elizabeth thought it a splendid idea, so we all agreed. The tickets were sold at ten shillings each, guaranteeing a prize for every ticket. It created a buzz about London, and the sales were good to start. Even poor people bought them by coming together and buying a small share of one ticket. Each ticket was blank so the buyer could sign their name and a unique line of verse or prayer to ensure they could be identified when they came to claim their prize.

London was crowded every day, and it was difficult for me and others to get about, especially around the cathedral. Entire villages had come into the city to witness the draw alongside wealthier people, and the crowds outside the west wing of St. Paul's stretched back as far as the eye could see. It had not been the greatest of successes, and only 40,000 of the 400,000 tickets had been sold.

I worked out that, after hours of standing, and because of the number of tickets sold, the people would have to attend the draw every day until their ticket was pulled from the box. The value of the prizes seemed so high it was worth standing in the icy winds each day for some. But the poorest were unhappy, and I heard them grumbling wherever I went, about how the lottery had been organised, having to leave because of the fear of losing their jobs or homes if they were away from work for too long.

*

I heard the gossip wherever I went. In the city and ports, all and sundry cursed Cecil's name as business came to a standstill, and traders feared it would estrange England from Spain and get into an alliance with France. In the country as a whole, Cecil had forfeited the goodwill of ordinary folk for his mishandling of the public lottery.

Knowing it was vital to calm things down, I met with my ally and ex-father-in-law, Henry Fitzalan, Earl of Arundel, and a staunch Catholic who supported Mary. We made it our business to contact the Spanish Ambassador, who had been confined to his house under guard since the Spanish ships had been taken. We sent the Florentine Banker Ridolfi to visit and assure him that the treasure ships would eventually be returned to Spain by Her Majesty. As we were not yet strong enough to resist Cecil, we gathered friends and let the public know what was going on, hoping and believing we could turn out the existing government and raise another.

It disappointed me that after our agreement, for which I was now taking action, Leicester seemed slow to declare himself. The others who had joined me intended to charge Cecil with being an 'evil advisor' in the Queen's absence and send him to the Tower.

Elizabeth and Cecil caught wind of the plan and summoned a Privy council meeting, but everyone who counted, even Leicester, made excuses for why they could not attend.

On Ash Wednesday, however, when I and my younger brother Henry and William Cecil had gathered in the Queen's Chamber, Leicester interrupted us. He stormed in and immediately rebuked Cecil in front of us all.

'You, my Lord, are ruining the State in the eyes of the people. The country no longer trusts the government, which turns them against our precious sovereign, the Queen. You are an evil advisor to Her Majesty and do encourage her in foul ways and deeds that anger her people.'

Elizabeth was furious. 'How dare you enter my privy Chamber thus, showing no deference to me or my lord Cecil? I will not have you speak to him in so vile a manner. Apologise immediately or suffer the consequences of your behaviour.'

I determined to support Leicester on this matter and turned to my brother before commenting conspiratorially but loud enough for the Queen to hear. 'You see, my Lord, how the Earl of Leicester is favoured only so long as he supports the Secretary, but now, for good reasons, he takes an opposed opinion; she frowns upon him and wants him sent to the tower.'

My brother replied in dramatic fashion, 'No, no, he will not go alone. I praise God that you, the first subject of the realm, are willing at last to show your quality. I am prepared to follow you and to support you in every way I can, for I have also come to complain.'

Elizabeth flushed with rage and ordered us all from her Chamber. I had hoped Leicester's planned interruption would open up a debate about Cecil's poor handling of the previous month's lottery and the damage he had caused through his treatment of the Spanish treasure ships. Now, I wondered if we had gone too far, but could not relent in my total dislike of Cecil, who had an even tighter hold on my sovereign than Leicester. Something had to be done to restore the devastation in trade he had caused.

A few days later, I received a letter from my closest friend, Sussex, in York. He seemed worried about me and Cecil becoming estranged, and offered to ride to London as our mediator. I replied, thanking him for the offer, but saying his journey was unnecessary and matters were in hand.

The following day, I received a note from Mary's Secretary, Maitland, with whom I had enjoyed a day's hawking while in York. He asked me to join him for a meeting to discuss the matter of his mistress. I arrived to find Throckmorton, a keen supporter of Mary, and Leicester there already.

'Come, Norfolk,' said Maitland, smiling and offering me a large glass of wine. 'We are discussing how to solve the current state of affairs. Most caused by Cecil, with his continual misguidance of Her Majesty Elizabeth, but also the matter of my mistress, the Queen of Scots. There is mounting discord about her treatment among the people of both Scotland and England.'

'The man is beyond suffering,' said Leicester, taking his usual vain stance that made him appear to be looking down his nose at everyone. 'The Queen doth hang on his every word, and his utter dislike of Mary is like to bring the country to civil war.'

I had always thought Leicester an arrogant man. Even with all that, I could not disagree with Leicester's statement. I looked to Maitland.

'Have we enough support to do something about Cecil and bring a safe conclusion to Mary's future whilst still ensuring loyalty to Her Majesty?'

Maitland answered, saying, 'We are of one accord you should marry Mary. It would satisfy the common people and the Catholic Earls both in England and Scotland. I fear if any harm should come to her, the result would be a bloody civil war. Moreover, we must bring about the downfall of Cecil afore we lose Spain as a trusted ally.'

I was quick to reply. 'I will do nothing that would harm my sovereign, and my agreement to the match would only be to benefit Elizabeth.'

Throckmorton quickly offered himself as my go-between, and we settled the matter.

Although I knew Leicester was only on my side because it could benefit his own plans of marrying Elizabeth, it was for just that reason I was relieved to have him as an ally.

We discussed the matter with the Bishop of Ross and opened negotiations with Regent Moray in Scotland. We suggested that the cancellation of Mary's abdication should be included in their terms. Once restored to her throne, Mary was to ratify the treaty of Edinburgh, and the Parliament at Westminster would then pronounce her heir presumptive to the throne of England.

I was hesitant, but my ambition and anger at Elizabeth's treatment of me and fear for Mary made me act. Whatever the outcome of Leicester's courtship, I could be assured of being King Consort in Scotland.

Leicester told us he aimed to carry the Council with him in order to force the issue with the Queen.

Chapter 5

April to June 1569

By April, the conspiracy to remove Cecil had lost its force; the Queen ignored all warnings and reasons placed before her and supported Cecil throughout, raging at her Councillors for their ill-treatment of him. It seemed not to matter what evidence we placed before her. She would heed no warnings and threatened the privy councillors with dismissal if they continued in their endeavours to remove him.

I was, nonetheless, delighted that, by then, several of the Council had rallied around me to promote my marriage to Mary. The Spanish Ambassador reported to all those involved with the marriage idea that Leicester had said he would tell the Queen and gain her approval.

Delays gave Cecil a chance to uncover our design. He confronted both myself and the Council at the next meeting and begged us not to do anything scandalous, saying, 'I will come over to your wishes on the marriage plan on the condition you stand by me and offer a united front to Spain.'

The meeting was in uproar. Angry at Cecil's audacity, I stood up to challenge him. 'You must end this hostile policy towards Spain. It is this that causes such unrest in our country. We cannot afford to lose our closest friend and ally. I will go to Spain gladly and smooth the waters if you wish, but I will not support your position. The treasure must be returned as I and my fellow councillors have requested so many times without answer.'

Over the next few days, Arundel and I continued to offer to go to Spain and try to make peace with King Philip, but Cecil denied permission, and it came to nothing. It angered me that this upstart could control my actions.

Meanwhile, I was encouraged by the fact that Leicester's scheme of persuading the Queen in favour of me marrying Mary still gained support in the Council, with the numbers in favour growing daily. I had, by now, actually exchanged tokens with Mary, and it looked like a promising union. Hopefully, Leicester would approach Elizabeth soon to gain her consent.

*

At the beginning of May, desperate to relax with my family at our home in Thetford, I left London. I had barely been there a day or two, when, after a morning with all my children in the nursery playing games with the younger ones before sitting down to a hearty dinner, I made my excuses to go to my study and write a letter to Leicester, as I was keen to know of his Progress.

Within minutes, I heard screams coming from the upper floors, and a servant burst into my room without waiting for instruction to enter.

Her face was white, as if she had suffered a great shock. She sobbed as she spoke.

'Come. Sire. Please come. Master George - the vaulting horse has fallen upon the poor child, and we cannot wake him.'

I raced past her and took the stairs two at a time. That boy would not be told. He was so fierce about all he did. George lay on the floor, still partway beneath the large vault, blood oozing from his mouth and head. I knelt beside him and stroked his face. 'George,' I whispered. 'Can you speak?' He did not answer, nor did he open his eyes. Looking to see what may have caused the accident, I saw a large iron pin next to the horse's back legs. George must have tried to remove it and lower the height to suit him. God's blood! How often had he been told he was too small to climb onto the horse?

'Send for a physic,' I screamed at a manservant before lifting my stepson and cradling his limp body. I carried him slowly downstairs and laid him on a couch before sending for warm water and a linen cloth so that I might clean his wounds. Meanwhile, I whispered to him, promising a pony if he would but open his eyes and speak to me. 'Listen to me, George. Your mother would not wish you to join her alongside her maker yet. You have a whole life to live. You and my little Megg will make the handsomest of couples when you are grown. Do not leave her all alone.'

It was an hour or more later when the physic arrived, but George's face had lost all colour by then. He had not spoken, and his small body did not move.

The entire house was in mourning for days before and after the funeral. All the children cried relentlessly, and nought I did could soothe them. I retreated to my study to grieve alone, praying to God and George's dead mother for forgiveness for letting such a thing happen to her only son.

*

I had stayed some weeks with the children. Trying to comfort them over their sad loss, and it was mid-June when Henry Fiennes invited me, along with my brothers-in-law, Lord Scrope, who was married to my sister Margaret, and Lord

Berkeley, my sister Katherine's husband, among others, to join him for a day's hawking at Clinton Estate, Tattersall. The company of my friends and family lifted my spirits after weeks of tension and sadness back at Thetford.

The sport done; I could not think of a better way to spend a warm summer's afternoon than in the countryside. We gathered together for refreshments and sat beneath a large tree. I sighed with contentment, breathing in the heady scent of summer flowers and thinking how exhilarating the sport had been, the day's memories dancing through my mind.

There was talk about my plan to marry Mary, all supporting the move to curtail Mary's hopes of taking the English throne.

'I am still hoping for Leicester to pave the way. He has promised to broach the subject with Her Majesty.'

'Strange bedfellow, Thomas. I thought you despised the pompous ass?' said Fiennes.

'I need him to convince the Queen. Regardless of my opinion of him, he holds the key to me getting her blessing.'

'And Cecil? Does he support your plan?' asked Scrope.

'Only if we support him in return and stop conspiring to get him removed from office. I would, I could do both, but I must now keep myself in his favour, or he will go against my plans.'

Upon finishing our refreshments and knowing we would soon part, we all stood and took a small branch from the tree and, hand in hand, took an oath to meet again for such a day every year hence.

Soon after the meeting, and back in London, I sent word to Mary, asking her to be cautious about sending letters from Wingfield Manor, as our intentions needed to be kept private for now. I could not risk word getting back to Elizabeth until Leicester had spoken to her.

Mary ignored my request and signed herself "your assured Mary" whenever she wrote to me. I repeatedly reminded her of the danger, getting increasingly frustrated with her disregard for her and my safety. Of course, she was a proud woman and entitled, as a queen, to speak as she pleased. I admired her brave heart, but it would not help our cause by being so reckless. She continued to send me tokens of love, to which I reciprocated by sending similar tokens in return. When breaking my fast one morning, my secretary brought me a package. It was more significant than the usual packages that would contain a brooch, ring, or some other personal item of Mary's, and I was curious. It felt soft, and I opened it carefully. Inside was a cushion Mary had embroidered with her own hands, depicting her arms and a hand with a pruning knife cutting down a green vine. She had stitched a motto into the cushion in Latin. "Virescit vulnere virtus" – "Virtue flourishes from its wounds". My heart beat in fear as I realised the Vine symbolised Elizabeth. I began to wonder in what exactly I had embroiled myself and hoped my trust in Leicester was not in vain. The sooner I received Elizabeth's support, the sooner I could shake off this fear of discovery.

Chapter 6

Summer 1569

I UNWILLINGLY STAYED IN London that summer. I could not risk being out of touch with events. Though I longed to go home to Kenninghall in Norwich to see if my children were recovering from their grief, it was not an option until the air cleared and Elizabeth's permission for the marriage had been secured. I feared she might hear by a side wind, and after a merry evening with Leicester and Arundel at Bletchingley, I returned to Howard House.

The day after, Cecil sent word that he wished to speak with me. When I entered his Chamber, Cecil sat behind his desk and signalled for me to sit in the chair facing him. I did not like his imperious manner.

'I must tell you, Norfolk, that the Queen has been out of quiet. She hears many rumours about you and the Scottish Queen,' he said, opening the meeting without preamble. 'What say you?'

''Tis true,' I said, not shirking away from the truth. 'I have most of the Privy Council's backing and am waiting for Leicester to speak to the Queen for me. He delays too long and says he must wait for the right moment. I have said I would seek permission myself, but he bids me to let him speak first to Her

Majesty. The Council think it a sound plan to deal with Mary, saving Her Majesty from worrying about succession.'

Cecil looked grave. 'You must tell the Queen as soon as possible. Let Leicester step aside. She already hears the gossip and is angry. If you make a clean breast of it, she may forgive you, but I warn you, Thomas, she will never agree to your proposal.'

Being the most powerful man in England after my cousin, the Queen, who considered herself a prince, I felt slighted that this man would tell me what to do. 'We must wait a while. The proposal is to come from Scotland. Secretary Maitland is due in London any day now. He is at the convention in Perth to get an agreement to Mary's divorce from Bothwell. We will approach the Queen then.'

Cecil exhaled deeply and replied in a more measured tone. 'You are a fool, Norfolk if you think this proposal can work. The Scottish adulteress will never be allowed to remarry. Beg forgiveness of your sovereign now afore you find your head on the block. I tell you this as a friend. I would not see you locked away in the Tower, but I will take Her Majesty's side in all things.'

I thanked him for the advice but was still reluctant to act against Leicester. Particularly now I knew of her anger. Better Leicester paved the way.

*

Leicester and I waited for the whole of July in vain. Secretary Maitland had staked all on getting the convention at Perth to pronounce in favour of Mary's divorce from Bothwell. Word came that when Moray secured the motion's defeat, Maitland was arrested and accused of being an accomplice in Darnley's murder.

As soon as I got the news, I implored Leicester to give a lead himself, to which he agreed, but said he must wait for the right moment or the result would be disastrous. And so July gave way to August.

Wishing to test my strength in the Council, I raised the subject from a different angle at the next sitting. I proposed Mary should be set at liberty on the condition she married an Englishman. An overwhelming majority passed the motion and agreed to stand by me and to carry this resolution into effect.

'At last, we can confront the Queen with the fact that most of the Council are in favour of the match; she surely cannot oppose it now,' I said, speaking to Leicester as we retired from the meeting and made our way to Leicester's Chamber.

'It would seem so,' said Leicester. 'I will think on it.'

'What is there to think on?' I snapped. 'The motion is passed. The Council are in favour,' I was totally frustrated with the man's dallying. 'I would go myself if it does not sit easily with you.'

I walked away from this supposed ally. I missed my closest friend Sussex's guidance and had no one else to turn to. My alliance with Leicester was an uneasy one, merely a marriage of convenience in which vows were taken in order to be broken. The Earl of Pembroke, who said he backed me wholeheartedly, lacked any strength of purpose and was under Leicester's domination, doing whatever he was told. My relations with Cecil could never be the same after the intrigues of the past spring and my own part in trying to unseat the man, and I refused to commit myself to Mary until the Queen had made up her mind.

I wished I could visit York to see Sussex, but it was impossible. Instead, I sent a message saying that Arundel, Pembroke, and Leicester had earnestly moved me to the marriage and asked Sussex's advice as a friend.

Sussex responded quickly.

'My dear friend, I feel it is too late in the day for my opinions if Leicester has already moved you to this decision and too early for suggesting how you should proceed as I know not how the Queen doth feel about the matter. I am sorry I accepted the position in York and cannot guide you at this difficult time.'

Chapter 7

August 1569

By the start of August, the court had moved to Richmond, and I followed a day later, even more eager to settle the matter. I rode directly to Leicester's house on the Thames at Kew. Leaving my mount with a stable hand, a servant escorted me down to the riverbank where Leicester was fishing. Another manservant stood close by, holding a net. It irked me that the man could enjoy a day's fishing when he should be working towards an agreement with Elizabeth for the marriage.

'Shhh!' whispered Leicester, his finger to his lips and saying I should move back from the edge as my shadow cast upon the water. 'I have a large Perch nosing at my bait,' he added, smiling.

I did as I was bid and grudgingly waited a good ten minutes for Leicester to reel in the fish and hold it high as the servant caught it up in the net, removed the hook and placed the perch in a wicker basket where it writhed and wriggled and gasped its last breath. I could not help but feel much like that fish. I was dangling from Leicester's hook, and it seemed I could do nothing about it.

Leicester stood and brushed himself down. He was still smiling when he turned to me.

'Come, Norfolk. Let us go inside out of the sun,' he said, marching towards the large brick mansion passed down to him by his father, John Dudley. The house was close to Richmond Palace, where the Queen held court.

I followed Leicester into a great hall. We both sat by a large hearth where a fire was already blazing. It was still a little chill in the cavernous room, and even though the sun blazed outside, very little warmth and light penetrated inside. I leaned forward, raising my hands toward the flames. A servant came in, carrying a large jug of wine and two tankards.

'I have news,' said Leicester, and my heart hiccupped and missed a beat as I wondered how Leicester's meeting with the Queen had progressed. At Last! There would be some progress. 'I am afraid it is not good. Affairs have reached a critical stage, and some women at court have babbled to the Queen. She is now convinced that you and the Scottish Queen will proceed with the marriage without consulting her.'

I felt physically sick. Memories of my father's imprisonment in the Tower and subsequent execution paralysed me with fear. I felt like the small child who had been left with nightmares about the torture and suffering my father must have experienced. I had dreamed almost every night of my father's head rolling down Tower Hill for years. I was not a coward when it came to defending my Queen and country. I would lay down my life in battle. It was the absolute terror of being locked up in the Tower, powerless and without a means of defence. How had Leicester allowed this to happen?

'You said you would speak to her. God's Blood, man!' I yelled, standing up so quickly that I spilt wine all down the front of my doublet. The servant flew across the room and dabbed at the stain with a scrap of linen. I batted him away. 'I need to speak to her immediately.'

Leicester waved his hand at me, showing that I should sit again. 'I have spoken to her. There is no need to fear. I have satisfied her that such tales were false. She is calmed for now, but we must tread warily and pick our time most carefully afore speaking to her on the topic again.'

'God's Blood! Why did you dither? Would it not have been a perfect opportunity?' I could hardly believe what he was saying.

'It was my head on the block at that moment. I have never seen her so angry. I could not. I give you my word. I will speak to her again soon. Now sit with me and relax. Have some more wine.'

He was right, of course. I could only hope Leicester would speak soon. I dare not approach her myself while her temper raged. Her tendency to lash out in anger without considering the consequences was what I feared most.

*

The Queen gave me a chance to speak to her a day before the court left Richmond. I had just returned from Howard House and was in the garden talking to the Marshall of the Berwick garrison about the State of the Scottish border when Elizabeth noticed me and called me to her side.

'What news has my cousin to tell me?'

I dithered, not knowing what to say, but remembering that Leicester had insisted I leave it to him, I stuttered as I answered, 'There is nothing to report, Your Majesty.'

'No! You come from London and tell no news of a marriage?'

I swallowed hard, pausing to ensure my words would not draw her. My mouth became dry as my mind whirled and spun, searching for the right words to bring everything out into the open. Just then, Lady Clinton came up with some flowers. Rather than wait and say my piece when the lady withdrew, I slunk off as a coward might to Leicester's rooms. After the Queen's hint, I was dumbfounded by Her Majesty's pleasant tone and determined to persuade the Earl of Leicester to let me tell her myself. Leicester was out stag hunting, but I patiently waited for him at his apartments. When he finally returned, I told him I had decided to speak to the Queen myself.

Leicester pounced before I had time to have my say fully. 'You cannot do that. It is too risky. We could lose everything for which we have planned.' Leicester now had a look of panic on his face. 'I have to pave the way. I cannot risk her thinking I was plotting behind her back. My future is also at risk.' He gripped my forearms. 'Be patient. You cannot jump in and risk our ruin. I promise to speak to her soon.'

As a result, I did as I was bid yet again, but Leicester had done nothing to move things forward and to obtain her permission by the time she left Richmond for her summer Progress. I disliked Progresses but had to follow to keep Leicester to his promises. After a few days at Oatlands Manor at Weybridge, Elizabeth journeyed to Guildford. Then she spent two days at Loseley, with Sir William More, at his fine new house at Guildford Park.

Becoming desperate, I spoke earnestly again to Leicester, and the following day, as I was passing the room that was being used as the privy Chamber, I found Her Majesty sitting on the threshold of the door. Leicester knelt by her as she listened to one of Sir William's children playing a lute and singing. The scene made me wish even more to be at Kenninghall with my children.

'Come Norfolk. You may join us.'

I obeyed Her Majesty and went in, sitting quietly and waiting for instruction. It was not long afore Leicester rose and came to me, leaving the Queen listening to the child. He whispered conspiratorially, 'I am currently dealing with Her Majesty on your behalf.'

I felt a twitch of fear and excitement rise within me. 'I see. If I had known so much, I would not have come in. Still, I desire to know how you find Her Majesty.'

'Her Highness has promised to speak to you at Thornham.' I was sorely disappointed. Arundel's house was in Kent, and the party would not arrive there until much later in the Progress. I wasn't sure my nerves could stand the waiting much longer.

*

When we reached Farnham, the Queen requested I alone should dine with her at her table, and at the end of the meal, she asked again. 'Are you sure there is nothing you need to say to me, Thomas?'

What to say? If I speak afore Leicester does, would we both end up in the Tower? He had seemed desperate to approach the Queen in such a way as would find us both in her favour. I found myself unable to speak about the affair once again, partly out of timidity, partly for fear of upsetting Leicester's plans. What approach had Leicester adopted back at Farnham? What if he now spoke and gave a different story? I had not conferred with him since the Queen's invite that morning, as Leicester had been away all day. 'There is nothing,' I said lamely, angry with myself at my lack of substance.

I realised Her Majesty had given me three opportunities to speak in the last ten days, but I had let them all slip by. There was no excuse for me remaining tongue-tied, and I had given the Queen every reason to think I had forfeited her confidence. I scolded myself, ashamed of my own cowardice. Why, I wondered, had I listened to Leicester in the first place?

We continued on Progress, reaching Southampton in leisurely stages, but after a day there, I returned to London, leaving both Leicester and even Cecil, who had now promised to speak to the Queen for me.

I prayed they would keep their word as I was now desperate, having received bad news from Moray in Scotland, who said he would not support the marriage.

Chapter 8

September to October 1569

I FELT MORE AT ease away from court, and my mood improved
when I received a letter from Pembroke saying that Elizabeth
dared not refuse her permission to the marriage as there was not a
person about her who dared give her contrary advice. My children
and stepchildren were staying at Philip's London home, Arundel House, with their nursemaid, Jane Goodman, and I visited
them as soon as I got back to London. Philip had married my
stepdaughter Nanne Dacre earlier in the year, but they remained
under supervision as they were still not of the age of consent.

Most of the work I had done in previous years at Howard
House had been for my beloved Margaret and, of course, to
make it in readiness for Elizabeth, who liked to stay occa-
sionally at the house where she had set off in procession to
her coronation in 1558. The extensive works had included
sumptuous living quarters, tennis courts, and a bowling alley.
The monk's refectory had been enlarged and adopted as a mag-
nificent hall where I had made the ceilings higher and had
installed an oriel window and a minstrel's gallery. I had built
a long gallery that ran east to west on the north side of the
hall, making communications easier between my private suite
in the west wing and the rooms in the east.

While back in London, I received a letter from the Earl of Northumberland, Thomas Percy, to say he intended to rescue Mary from Shrewsbury's custody at Wingfield and that the whole of the North was at his devotion. Glad at last for some support of my plan to marry the Scottish Queen, I approved the project, thinking that, once free and staying with Percy, Elizabeth would more likely agree to my wedding the Scottish Queen.

My ease lasted little more than a day when I received a letter from Cecil from the Vine near Basingstoke. Cecil told me I must hasten to court as the Queen had asked for me. Cecil said he could no longer support my plans to marry Mary, as some members of the court, particularly Baron Hunsdon, were now speaking out against the match. I could hardly believe things had turned around so quickly. Had Pembroke had his ears closed to any protests? I sent an urgent message to Leicester, asking him to speak to the Queen afore it was too late. Meanwhile, I could not refuse my sovereign's command, and so travelled south, biding my time while awaiting the summons I knew would come.

It was not long on the journey before I received a message to say that Leicester had taken to his bed at Titchfield, the Earl of Southampton's mansion. My heart sank. Leicester, when most needed, had shrunk away once more.

I arrived at Titchfield the following day and was immediately summoned to the Queen's chambers. As I entered the room, I kept my head low and appeared as humble as I might be. Elizabeth was dressed top to toe in cloth of gold, her face beautifully white and her lips rouged, her hair almost the same colour as her dress, but her eyes were hard and piercing.

'So! At last, he comes.'

'My Lady—'

'I will speak Norfolk. You, Sir, will listen. I have come this day from Leicester's sickbed.' I swallowed hard. 'He has told me all of your plans to marry the adulteress and assures me of his loyalty and how you cajoled him into agreeing to support you. He now understands why it was ill-thought-out and has begged my forgiveness. You, on the other hand, have been given many opportunities to confess your intentions and have stoutly denied them at every turn.'

'My Lady, I beg you, listen... It was not—'

'Silence. Do not interrupt your Queen when she is speaking. I will tell you when I wish to hear from you. The time for friendly warnings has passed. I charge you on your allegiance to deal no further with the Scottish cause. My mind will have no leeway should you fail me in this.'

I dared to look at her, trying to show a penitent face of shame and sadness. I did the only thing I could think of to escape her wrath. 'I promise faithfully to give over any pretensions of making Mary my wife, as I have very slight regard for her. I realise my mistakes and even her position, were it to be restored, is of no attraction to me.' Her eyes softened slightly, my confidence grew, and I let my mouth speak more confidently with pride. 'Indeed, my own revenues are not much less than those of the Kingdom of Scotland, and when I am in my tennis court at Norwich, I sometimes think of myself in a manner equal with some kings.'

As soon as the words were out of my mouth, I wished I could swallow them and imprison them inside my head.

*

I did not escape from court immediately, knowing it would raise suspicion as to my intentions, so I continued with the Progress, but courtiers began to shun me.

'I am right sorry,' I told Cecil a couple of days later. 'that no man can keep me company without offence. I never deserved to be so ill-thought of. I hope time will bring her Majesty to like of them which wish best to herself, and till then, I must bear all over warts with patience.'

Each day became more uneasy. No other peer joined me at the table; everyone whispered about me, and worst of all, Leicester treated me with icy disdain. He had betrayed me, and I could do little about it.

At last, I could stand it no longer and left without seeking formal leave to depart from court. Instead, I let it be known I needed to be in London for some days to prepare for some lawsuits coming up in the Michaelmas term.

A servant of my brother Henry met me as I left Titchfield and suggested in all seriousness that we should take the Tower, but I thought it a monstrous idea. On the way home, I called in at Wilton to speak to Pembroke, who I hoped could still influence the Queen, but he thought it was now useless. I found no peace in London either, with too many rumours regarding my safety.

Cecil sent me a message, which alarmed me enough to make my whole being shake with fear. My terror of being imprisoned surfaced once more as I read the words.

'Elizabeth worries that your sudden departure might be the prologue to a general rising, which would bring all the opponents of her regime under one banner. She thinks you would rescue Mary from Wingfield and advance on London. She fears your actions will instil Northumberland and Westmorland to rise and bring about a civil war. The Queen will have Mary removed from Wingfield to somewhere safer. She has bid me write to you and order you to repair to Windsor where she is now and be ready to submit to her.'

In responding to Cecil, I pleaded an ague; it was not a lie. I told him I did not wish to risk travelling until the attack was quite over, but that I hoped to be at Windsor as soon as I was able.

A letter from Leicester arrived at Howard House a day or two later, warning me I may be sent to the Tower. That night, Lumley and Bishop Ross called to offer advice, Ross bringing a ring as a token from Mary, but it gave me little comfort. My courage failed me, and rather than face the Queen, I rode off the following night to Kenninghall.
Once at home, I wrote to Elizabeth.

'My enemies found such comfort in your Highness's heavy displeasure that they made of me a common table talk; my friends were afraid of my company, and it became unbearable. I came home to take to my bed with an ague. I am not well and did not intend alarm.'

The County's leaders came to pay court to me within a day or two, as was usual when I was at Kenninghall. They were unaware I had been shunned at court, and I was not about to tell them. Were these men rallying to my cause? They had all been angry of late as the closure of the traditional markets for English cloth on the continent, through Alva's advance in the Netherlands, had caused a crisis in the clothing industry. Huguenot settlers caused bitterness in Norwich by over-saturating the market. A vigorous attempt to enforce the Acts of Supremacy and Uniformity was, for the first time, seriously embarrassing those Catholics who could hitherto wink at the law.

Elizabeth's letter in reply to me, as soon as she heard I had gone home, commanded me on my allegiance to repair to Windsor without delay in the company of the bearer of the letter, Edward Fitzgarret, a gentleman pensioner. I read the last line with dread,

'I have no intention of ministering anything to you, but as you should in truth deserve.'

I refused to accompany Fitzgarret, pleading great illness.

I now knew that I had become a suspected person and saw the shadow of the Tower hanging over me. I wrote to what was left of my friends.

'I have but withdrawn to procure a remedy against indignant rumours, which are always entertained at court'.

The next day, I received a message from Leicester.

'When Elizabeth heard on the 26th of you leaving London, she did not realise it was a retreat but imagined it as the signal for rebellion. Everyone at court thought you had ridden north and not to Kenninghall. Arundel and Pembroke are under house arrest, and Lumley is summoned to court. The court is in suspense and fear lest you break forth into a rebellion, and Cecil has been ordered that Mary should be put to death if you do so.'

Then I heard from my sister, Jane, who was married to the Earl of Westmorland, that I was expected to lead a movement which would put the clock back in religion and politics, a rising not so much against the Crown but its evil advisors. They promised me full support if I needed it, and they meant it. They urged me not to count on Elizabeth's goodwill but on their assistance to the utmost of their power. I could not believe what I was reading as I scanned the last lines of the letter.

'Christopher Norton is ready to ride off into the night to rescue Mary under the colour of another of her ladies, whom he professed to love. We will kill Knollys, John Forster and even Regent Moray for his betrayal of you.'

Fear paralysed me. Everyone was making their own assumptions about my intentions. I had intended neither rebellion nor to go against my Queen, but to offer her and the people a way forward without revolution or bloodshed. I immediately sent a messenger to Percy at Topcliffe, in the North of the country, to ask the northern earls to call off their projected rising, to reiterate I had only supported them rescuing Mary, and to impress upon them that if they did rise, it would cost me my head. I prayed they would heed me.

I lay in bed, ill with ague, my body racked with pain, all probably brought on by my worry over the past few weeks. I had withdrawn from court, furious that my immediate hopes of marrying Mary had been dashed and for fear of being put in the Tower. I remembered again the horrors my grandfather had told me of being in the Tower for several years. My head was filled with a picture of my father being taken to Tower Hill. I buried my head into my pillow to stifle the wails that burst forth from me.

*

The following day, Fitzgarret arrived again with a letter from the Queen and was escorted directly to my bedside.

Exhausted from lack of sleep and relentless pain, I read the letter. The Queen now stated that sickness was no valid excuse, and, regardless of my health, I was to set out for Windsor, use a Litter if necessary and make the journey in easy stages. She warned me I must now come to her and demonstrate the loyalty and humility I constantly professed. Fitzgarret also carried a message from Cecil, who wrote, too, saying that Elizabeth's counsel was very earnest and straight and trusted that I would endure nothing more harmful than words – at the most, to be forbidden to come to her presence, as in the cases of Arundel and Pembroke.

'I would be left alone awhile to think on Her Majesty's words,' I said weakly. 'Take leave of me, and I will dress presently.' My manservant escorted Fitzgarret from the bedchamber.

I was too afraid to do anything as I lay on my bed, wondering what would become of me and my family, when a manservant brought yet another missive.

I recognised the writing of my former tutor and dearest friend, John Foxe.

'I am astounded at the rumour in almost every man's mouth. You must be circumspect. If you hoped to marry Mary, you would ruin both yourself and your country. There is no greater cunning in these days than to know whom a man may trust; examples you have enough within the compass of your own days, whereby you may know what noblemen have been cast away by them whom they seemed most to trust. Remember, I pray you, the example of Mephibosheth, whereof I told you being young.'

Edward Clere, member of parliament for Thetford, having heard of the rumours and the Queen's anger, came to pay his respects later that day and enquire about my health and my intentions. I still had not risen from my bed, the ague becoming worse. I welcomed Clere and discussed what I now saw as my only options.

'I have three,' I said. 'The first is to accompany Fitzgarrett, go to Windsor, and submit to the Queen. The second to depart the realm and live quietly abroad or thirdly, to stand upon my guard, the last thing I expected to do.'

Clere looked down at me, his eyes full of sympathy. 'You know, the only honourable course is to go to court. You could never live as an expatriate, and if it needs courage to stand at the head of an army of insurgents, it also requires courage to take your life into your own hands and submit to Her Majesty.'

In the end, I swallowed my fear and pride and decided to throw myself upon Elizabeth's mercy. Crumpled and bowed, I set off for Newmarket with Fitzgarrett, accompanied by thirty of my retainers. As the party left Kenninghall, I glanced back, knowing I might never set eyes on this beautiful home again. When our party reached St Albans, I sent word of my impending arrival at court to my staff and asked them to prepare my usual lodgings. That evening, Lawrence Bannister, good friend and trustee for the Dacre Estate, brought a message warning me that, instead of going to Windsor, I was to be taken to Paul Wentworth's house at Burnham and urging me to devise a scheme for passing letters.

The following afternoon, Fitzgarret escorted me into Wentworth's house. Once there, I discovered the Queen had appointed Henry Neville as my keeper with instructions to remove various of my servants, deny me any visitors, and see that no letters passed.

I attempted passing messages inside bottles, but Neville soon discovered what I was doing.

The Queen ordered the Sheriff of Norfolk to arrest some twenty retainers and other servants of mine and send them to Windsor for cross-examination, in particular Sir Nicholas L'Estrange, Robert Higford, William Barker, and Lawrence Bannister.

After eight nights at Burnham, Sir Francis Knollys took me to the Tower, though Neville was to have special charge of me. They escorted me to a room in the Constable's lodging, which my grandfather had occupied for six years. I shivered as I remembered all my grandfather had told me.

I learned through Neville that Pembroke, Arundel, and Lumley had been questioned a week earlier. Then, in October, they and Throckmorton were examined again more thoroughly.

'Interminable questions were asked of the Bishop of Ross,' he said, a triumphant smile upon his face, 'and Mary has had all her papers ransacked.'

I also heard through Neville that Leicester had gone on his knees, told all he knew and received absolution, though he received some censure for his part, but said he only had a foot in Norfolk's camp to keep himself informed. I cursed myself for ever having trusted the man, astonished at my gullibility and stupidity.

Nell, one of only two servants allowed me, was employed in the Tower kitchens, bringing my meals and clean washing daily. For little coin from faithful friends, she sneaked in messages by memorising them or secreting them amongst the leathern medication bottles. Through them, I discovered that Elizabeth had pressed Moray, by special messenger, to procure as many proofs as he could to show that I had first suggested the marriage to him and not vice versa. One letter that escaped detection told me that Regent Moray had said he could not oblige Her Majesty and had written a long account, blaming Secretary Maitland. Moray also, which was not good news, had sent down his own secretary to the Queen to give her all the letters he had received from me.

I also learned from my keeper Knollys that when Sussex heard I was under suspicion, he had implored Cecil to do what he could to persuade Elizabeth that I was an innocent conspirator.

'He is as good a friend as can be,' I said, my hope rising a little.

Knollys raised a hand to quiet me. 'Sadly, the Queen and Cecil have not been satisfied with Sussex's views as they are not sure that he is acting vigorously enough in the North. They have pressed him again regarding his loyalty. They fear the North would be lost if he sides with the northern Earls.

Sussex has sworn he had only replied to you, saying that his consent to the marriage hinged on Elizabeth's approval and that he had always hitched his staff at her door.'

I sighed. I could not deny it. Sussex had advised me thus.

By mid-November, I heard the news that Northumberland and Westmoreland had marched to Durham Cathedral, thrown out the Dean and held a catholic mass. The Earls were now marching south and intended to free Mary. The Queen had sent a large army north to meet them.

I shook with fear and anger at the news. I had begged them not to rise. Their rebellion would help the Queen's cause in charging me with treason.

I asked for pen and paper so that I might write to my children, knowing I would never see them again. My request was refused, and I knelt to pray.

'Please, God, let my end be swift and fetch me to my past wives, who I miss much. Keep all my children safe, give them long and happy lives and help them make wise decisions and not follow the path of their foolish father.'

You CAN FOLLOW THIS brief prologue of the lead-up to The Northern Rebellion by reading THE RIPPON SPURRIER (Book One of Tudor, treason and Plot). Available on Amazon at:

https://a.co/d/jbL0CKH   or
https://amzn.eu/d/0wwT5yw

Acknowledgements

I WANT TO THANK my family for all their support over the years, especially my husband John, for his unlimited patience and the hours he spends proofreading my books, and my children for encouraging me to keep going.

Second, my treasured writing group, The Next Chapter, without whom I would be lost. They always keep me on the straight and narrow with their help, encouragement, and attention to detail.

I want to send a big thank you to Jackie Buxton, who never fails to spur me on.

Last but certainly not least, I would like to thank The LWS Writers Salon Zoom group for supplying me with a writing space up to four times a day and the great group of friends I have made there, and from whom I can ask for advice whenever needed.

Bibliography

Williams, N. (1964). *A Tudor Tragedy* (1st ed., p. 289). Barrie & Jenkins.

Edwards, F. (1968). *A Marvellous Chance* (1st ed., p. 416). Rupert Hart-Davis Ltd.

Printed in Great Britain
by Amazon

49550697R00033